EXECUTIVE ONE FOXTROT

DON'T MISS THESE ALEX ANDER THRILLERS!

Alex Ander writes what he enjoys reading – action thrillers packed with fistfights, gunfights, good-and-decent main characters, and heart-pounding excitement and adventure...all with clean language, no graphic sex, and an undertone of faith from a Christian worldview.

Aaron Hardy – Ex-Special Forces

The Unsanctioned Patriot

American Influence

Deadly Assignment

Patriot Assassin

The Nemesis Protocol

Necessary Means

Foreign Soil

Of Patriots and Tyrants

Act of Justice

The Last Kill

Two Minutes to War

Three Days in Rome

Dark Days of the Republic

Act of War

BIG SKY Series – Sheriff Wade Lockhart

Big Sky

Ambush

Reckoning

Jacob St. Christopher – Former FBI Hostage Rescue

Protect & Defend
Word of Honor
A Vow to the Innocent
Above & Beyond
Hard Road to Redemption

Jaxon Reigns – Ex-CIA Paramilitary Operations

To Reign Supreme
Hard Reign

Special Agent Cruz – FBI Agent

Vengeance is Mine
Defense of Innocents
Plea for Justice

Jessica Devlin – U.S. Marshal

Trust Fall
No Good Options
Let the Hunt Begin

Other Action Thrillers

Kill Order
Far From Mercy
Executive One Foxtrot

FREE Ebook
Escape & Evade
Go to AlexAnderNovelist.com

EXECUTIVE ONE FOXTROT

A PATRIOTIC THRILLER

ALEX ANDER

TABLE OF CONTENTS

"I command you: be strong and steadfast!
Do not fear nor be dismayed,
for the Lord, your God,
is with you wherever you go."
~ Joshua Chapter 1; Verse 9

EXECUTIVE ONE FOXTROT

9 NOVEMBER—5:37 P.M.
50 MILES NORTHEAST OF
PANAMA CITY, PANAMA

The weight bearing down on the First Lady of the United States was suffocating, like being at the bottom of the pile after a fourth-and-inches goal line stand. She had never considered herself claustrophobic. But having been shoved to the Chevy Suburban's floorboards between the backseat and the front seat's upright, her left cheek pressing on a dirty floor mat, FLOTUS was now having second thoughts about that self-assessment. Plus, the two-hundred-plus-pound man pinning her to the floor only added to her fears.

The speeding SUV hit a bump, forcing the man on top of her to rise into the air a fraction of an inch. She was able to steal a half breath before the heavyweight came back down again, the man's momentum compressing her upper body even more.

Moments ago, or *minutes* ago—since it's hard to tell time when you're struggling to breathe and can't see anything but carpet fibers and the metal workings beneath the driver's seat—the mad dash to the motorcade had been chaotic.

• • •

Minutes ago...

"In closing," said the First Lady, standing behind a makeshift podium and speaking to a small crowd of Panamanians who looked as ragged and worn out as the weather-ravaged countryside surrounding the gathering, "I'd like to take this opportunity to assure you, the citizens of Panama, that," she glanced at her hand-written remarks, "the United State—"

Deafening booms and ear-splitting cracks interrupted the speech, shattering the atmosphere of an otherwise peaceful evening.

Shouting and screaming, people ducked and ran for cover.

In an instant, FLOTUS was surrounded by men in black suits. A hand clamped around the back of her neck and pushed her head downward. Her notes went flying, and all the First Lady could now make out were the shiny dress shoes of her Secret Service detail. In fact, she wasn't really sure she was even in control of her footsteps as the agents were seemingly carrying her.

The barrage of gunshots continued unceasingly, coming from all directions.

FLOTUS heard the shouts, the cries of civilians caught in the crossfire, the grunts coming from the men around her. One by one, after each muffled groan, a pair of black dress shoes near her disappeared from her vision.

Twice her armed escorts veered off course and took cover—shielding FLOTUS with their bodies—only to yank her to her feet a second later, their pistols barking, as the diamond formation, with the First Lady in the center, rushed forward.

"Shooter—ten o'clock."

Gunfire.

"Three o'clock! Three o'clock!"

More gunfire.

"Threat down. Go, go, go!"

"Sunflower on the move."

"Eight o'clock. White truck. Front bum—" a loud groan came before a pair of shoes disappeared.

"Engaging."

Gunfire.

"Threat dow—" a moan came before another set of shoes disappeared.

"Robbins, take left flank," shouted the man 'glued' to the First Lady.

Shoes came into view on her left as she glimpsed an SUV up ahead.

"Fall back and—" her 'shadow' let loose with three rounds from his pistol.

The First Lady flinched every time the weapon fired.

"Fall back and establish perimeter."

Seconds later, her world went dark when she was pushed into the SUV and shoved face first to the floor, the man on her immediate left throwing himself on top of her. The vehicle was rolling before she saw the right-rear door slam shut.

• • •

Present time...

Now, several starts and stops and sharp turns later, with the Secret Service agent draped over her, crushing her upper body, FLOTUS did her best at a one-handed push-up. With her left arm wedged under her, she drove her left elbow downward. Both actions allowed her to gain some separation from the floor, and she grabbed a scant breath before gravity and lack of muscle strength once again forced her back down. Unable to fill her lungs, panic sunk in. Perspiration dotted her forehead. A deep thirst gripped at the back of her throat. And her chest felt like it was collapsing, as she labored for more oxygen, heck, *any* oxygen.

The SUV rolled to a halt then lurched backward a few seconds ahead of the left-rear door swinging open.

FLOTUS lifted her eyes to see another black-suited man wrestling with the one covering her. Seconds later, the heavy load was gone, and she rolled right to get her first full breath in who knows how long.

Strong hands slipped under her armpits.

Hoisted upward, she was dragged out of the vehicle, her chunky high heels scraping across the floorboards, before she was placed on her feet.

…

Ten seconds earlier...

The driver threw the gearshift into 'PARK,' pushed open his door, and clambered outside, his peripheral vision picking up on the smoke billowing from the front of the SUV while he drew his Glock G19 Gen5 MOS pistol. He opened the left-rear door, his head on a swivel, his eyes taking in every detail behind the boarded-up supermarket, wood coverings on windows being the owner's last-ditch attempt at saving his property from the tropical storm that had recently ravaged the area.

Moments later, he looked down to see a motionless Secret Service agent lying on the First Lady.

The prone man's black suit coat had two holes in it, two darker, circular patches growing wider.

The driver holstered his weapon then wrestled to roll his fellow agent onto the backseat. After checking the man for vital signs, and finding none, he slid his hands under the woman's armpits, hauled her out of the SUV, and gently set her on her feet. "Are you all right, Mrs. Conklin? Are you injured? Are you feeling any pain anywhere?" he said, all the while inspecting her for obvious signs of physical trauma.

Based on the powerful arms that had lifted her from the vehicle, Caroline Conklin had anticipated having to

ALEX ANDER 5

crane her neck at someone towering above her five-three height. Instead, she found herself only a couple inches shy of her rescuer. Granted, the difference was skewed by her three-inch black high heels, however.

The late-forties woman straightened her rumpled navy-blue pantsuit before unbuttoning the jacket to inspect her white blouse underneath. "I-I don't think so." She quickly ran fingers through her shoulder-length strawberry blonde hair, pushing aside the wavy locks that blocked her vision.

"Good." Removing his black sunglasses, the man took her by the right elbow and led her away from the disabled ride. "We should get going." With one hand, he folded the spectacles then stuffed them into a pocket on his black suit coat.

"Why not take the car?"

"It took a round in the radiator. It barely had enough power to get us this far."

The two fast walked toward the corner of the single-story building, Caroline's heels clicking and scuffing as she did her best to keep up with her guide's pace. She glanced back. "Where are the others? There were three cars in the motorcade."

"One vehicle was disabled. I'm not sure about the third."

Caroline frowned while recalling all the pairs of shoes that had disappeared from her vision during the race to the SUV. Her heart sunk when she turned back to see the motionless agent who had been lying on top of her. Knowing the answer to her next question, she asked anyway. "What," she faltered, "what about the others...the men who were with you?"

They made a hard left then navigated a narrow alley before emerging onto a sidewalk.

"Many of them fell during the gunfight," said the man. "Those left standing stayed behind to give us time to escape." The Secret Service agent dug out his cell phone and saw that he had no cellular service.

Caroline slowed and thrust out her left arm to steady herself on the building. A tick later, she bent over and put her free hand to her stomach.

The agent whirled around and dashed to her side. "Ma'am?"

She waved him off then wiped sweat from her forehead. "It's all right. I'm fine. I just," she swallowed, hoping to keep the bile in her throat from advancing any further, "I just suddenly feel sick to my stomach." She made a face and blinked several times, moisture gathering at the corners of her eyes. "All those men." She shook her head and sniffed before using her fingers to clear away the tears. "All those men."

"Those men would have died a *thousand* deaths to protect Sunflower. That's our job, our calling. It's what we're trained for."

Caroline heard the call sign that had been assigned to her. With her daughter's call sign being Red Rose, she was pleased that the Secret Service had stayed with the flower theme. And it just so happened that sunflowers were near the top of her list when it came to her favorites. "I know." Caroline nodded. "I know. But it's still hard to wrap my head around good people dying so that I might live." She sniffled again then swiped fingers over her nose.

His head spinning left and right, the agent retrieved a white handkerchief from a trouser pocket and held it out to her while looking up and repeating his scanning procedure.

Caroline accepted the offering. "Thank you."

"You're welcome, Ma'am." He continued surveying the empty street before glancing up to take in the upper windows and rooftops. "We need to keep moving, get off the street. I know a place, a block over, where we can hide for the time being."

She dried her eyes and nose with the cloth then nodded. "I'm ready."

He claimed her elbow again.

"Sorry for being such a wimp."

The two hurried forward.

"You're not a wimp, Ma'am. It's called having a big heart. And it's one of the reasons why I'm honored—why *all of us*—are honored to have the opportunity to safeguard you."

They jogged across the street.

Caroline threw out her right leg, half leaping for the

    EXECUTIVE ONE FOXTROT

curb and half trying to keep up with the agent. Her heel skidded over the raised concrete. Her right ankle twisted a bit, and she wobbled, her right knee buckling. "Oh, sh..."

He caught her as she finished her curse in his left ear. "I got you. You're good."

She regained her balance and half smiled at him. "I'm sorry. That wasn't very," a beat, "*first* ladylike of me."

"I've heard much worse, Ma'am." He dipped his chin at her. "You ready?"

She nodded.

The two fast walked down a narrow side street, dodging broken bottles, tipped-over trash cans, and a mound of something black and mushy to which both people gave a wide berth.

Veering right and stooping, the agent snagged a two-foot length of rusted pipe.

"What's that for?" asked Caroline, her brows coming together.

"I'm thinking I might need a persuader."

"A persuader?"

"We're almost there, Ma'am." Exiting the side street, he ushered her to the left then pulled on a door handle.

The door didn't budge.

"Stand back, Ma'am."

FLOTUS backtracked a couple feet.

On his second swing of the pipe, he shattered a window on the door. Using the steel conduit, he cleared away the rest of the shards, stuck an arm inside the opening, and unlocked the door. After stepping inside, he backed out and motioned. "After you, Mrs. Conklin. The way's clear."

She spied the 'persuader' he held then proffered a half grin while bypassing her protector. "From what I'm told, my husband could use a *persuasive* man like you at his cabinet meetings."

The agent surveyed the surrounding area. Satisfied no one was watching, he slipped into the building and shut the door.

The four-story office building was finished off but empty. The carpeting had been laid, the walls painted, and the tile ceiling installed. Everything was ready for the owners to start renting space. Then the earthquake had struck, and all business plans had come to a grinding halt.

"I'm not trying to tell you how to do your job, but," the First Lady rolled her head to glance at the white ceiling before her eyes shifted to the tan carpeting beneath her feet, "is it wise for us to be up here," a beat, "you know, since the earthquake and all?"

Standing at a bank of windows overlooking the street, the Secret Service agent studied the area below. "This is the newest building in Panama. Unlike a lot of the others, this one was built to modern specs." He glimpsed his questioner. "We're safe up here, Ma'am."

She rolled a chair out from under a cubicle desk and dropped onto the cushioned seat. A moment later, she leaned forward and laid her head on her palms, elbows on knees. *All those men.* A tick. *And their families.* Another moment. *How do you face the loved ones of those who died to—*

"Mrs. Conklin?"

She looked up while dragging her hands down her face, pausing to cover her mouth while she eyed him.

"Are you okay?"

She half closed an eye at him then barely nodded, "I'm fine," before sitting upright. "Forgive me."

"For what, Ma'am?"

"It just dawned on me. I don't even know your name. In fact, I don't think I've ever seen you before."

"That's because I'm kind of new to your detail. I'm not part of your inner circle of agents. My responsibilities include scouting the places you're going to as well as guarding the outer perimeter when you're on the move."

She nodded. "So, what *is* your name?"

"Agent Winchester."

"Well, Agent Winchester, thank you for all you've done."

"Just doing my job, Ma'am." Winchester went back to gawking out the window.

"Do you have family...girlfriend, wife, siblings?"

"Single." Distracted, he checked his phone. "Parents live in Minnesota." He made a face at not having a signal. "Two older sisters."

Caroline bobbed her head at the conciseness of his answers. *Not much of a talker, I see.* "Okay," she replied, her voice curt. "All business. I can appreciate that." She stood. "So, what's next? What do we do now?"

Winchester turned away from the glass to glimpse the one in his charge. "I'm sorry, Ma'am. I don't mean to be rude. I was hoping with us being higher up that I'd get some sort of signal."

"That's quite all right. It's been a tough day. I understand." A beat. "Change of topic. Who was shooting at us back there? It sounded like we were surrounded."

"We were. Gunfire was coming from all directions—pistols *and* rifles. As to the who, I can only speculate that it was one of any number of gangs here in Panama or the neighboring countries of Costa Rica or Columbia."

Caroline scrunched her nose. "Why would they want to attack me?"

He glanced out the window, taking in both ends of the street. "Kidnapping is a lucrative business if you snatch a wealthy businessman, the son or daughter of a wealthy businessman, or," he met her gaze and let his voice trail off.

"Or," she nodded, "a US President's wife." Caroline grimaced while massaging her forehead. "Maybe this trip was a mistake." A pulse. "But these people have been hit so hard. All I wanted to do was let them know that we see them, that the United States stands with them in their efforts to rebuild. I never meant to get anyone killed."

Winchester spun on his heels to face her. "You didn't get anyone killed. The ones pulling the triggers back there did the killing. Your only fault, Ma'am, is that you're a kind woman." He shook his head at her. "And that is *nothing* to be ashamed of."

The First Lady took a moment to compose herself.

"All right. What about the Panamanian police? Surely, they were alerted to the ambush and are doing something."

"Even if they're mobilizing right now, I'm not confident we can trust them."

She raised an eyebrow.

He noticed. "During the gunfight, I saw one of the Panamanian officers shooting at one of my colleagues. Now," Winchester shook his head once, "in all the confusion, I could be wrong, but if there's even the slightest chance the authorities have been infiltrated, or the enemy is dressing like them, impersonating them, then we can't count on the Panamanian police."

For the first time since being dragged from the SUV, Caroline noted how young this man looked. By her estimation, he couldn't be over thirty. Twenty-seven or twenty-eight, she guessed. His cheeks and chin were smooth, clean shaven, and showed no blemishes. His light-brown hair, bordering on blonde, was cut short, almost to crew cut length. Above his ears, the sides were even shorter. Finally, his bright-blue eyes knifed through the darkened office space. But despite his youthfulness, he had a commanding presence that betrayed his presumed inexperience.

Winchester tipped his head back to gape at the ceiling. "I need to get higher," he mumbled before facing the First Lady. *But I can't leave her alone.*

For a few moments, the two stared at each other.

He gave the street below a last look then peeled away from the windows, gently hooking her left elbow. "Please come with me, Ma'am."

"Where are we going?"

"Upstairs."

"Upstairs? I thought we were on the top floor already."

"There's one more." He opened a door and led her through the archway, up a flight of stairs, and through another door, both stepping onto a flat and tarred roof a tick later.

Air conditioning equipment, housed in a metal box, sat near the eight-foot-high, four-by-six-foot enclosure they had just exited. The rest of the roof was wide-open space.

The two strode to the side of the roof that faced the direction where the gun battle had taken place.

Winchester made sure his earpiece was secured in his left ear then raised his left arm and spoke into a device attached to his shirt's cuff. "This is Special Agent Remington Winchester."

Caroline frowned at the side of his face.

"Does anyone copy? Over."

Five seconds passed.

"This is Special Agent Remington Winchester. Does anyone copy? Over."

Three seconds.

Looking down, he reached between his jacket and his

shirt, turned a knob on his two-way radio, then repeated himself. Not getting a response, he filled his lungs and exhaled a big breath at the landscape before him. Most of the buildings were one story high. A few rose an extra story. Tall trees dotted the terrain, blocking out what would otherwise be an unobstructed view.

He pivoted his upper body to peer over his shoulder.

To the southeast, a hundred miles away, the Pan-American Highway ended at the Darién Gap. It picked up again sixty-six miles later, but in that gap lay a whole lot of rough, forested land.

He spun back, his mind showing him the Gulf of Panama and the Caribbean Sea to his left and right, respectively, plus more dense forests between him and the coastlines. And the two recent tropical storms had flooded many areas in this part of Panama. Whatever roads there were would most likely be impassable. No. His only way of getting to the First Lady's Boeing C-32A jet, waiting for her at Tocumen International Airport, in Panama City, was the Pan-American Highway, northwest of his position. That path, however, would take him and her straight toward the enemy.

Winchester rubbed the back of his neck while glimpsing the watch on his left wrist—5:57. *Sun sets in forty minutes.* He grimaced at the fading daylight. The thought of spending the night in an abandoned building with the President's wife, with armed men roaming about, made his stomach do backflips.

     EXECUTIVE ONE FOXTROT

"I'm sorry to interrupt," said Caroline. "I can see you have a lot on your mind, but my curiosity is getting the best of me." A beat. "Who's the gun enthusiast, your father or your mother?"

Frowning, Winchester turned to face his questioner. A moment later, he shut his eyes and nodded twice. "My parents took turns naming us. It was my dad's turn when I was born."

"Dare I ask what your middle name is?"

"I'm told my father wanted to name me Colt. But my mother, fearing there would not be a fourth child, didn't want her only son named after three different gun manufacturers."

Caroline nodded. "And?"

"And," Winchester paused, "they came to a compromise."

"Which was?"

"My middle name is," he paused, "Colton."

Picturing his full name, *Remington Colton Winchester*, FLOTUS sniggered. "Young man, I think your father may have still won that battle."

"I'm thinking he did, too."

Caroline's laughter died down. "May I call you Remington? Agent Winchester seems so impersonal, especially after the last half-hour's events."

"My family and friends call me Remi, but you can call me whatever you want, Ma'am."

"Thank you. Remi, it is. And about all the Ma'ams,"

she hesitated, "I want you to call me Caroline."

Winchester made a face while cocking his head. "With all due respect, I'm not sure I can do that. There's no way I'd call your husband James or Jim or Jimbo. His position commands respect. And that same respect certainly carries over to you, Mrs. Conklin."

"Well, how about this? Like your mother and father did, let's come to a compromise. I'll call you Remi, and you call me Caroline."

Winchester opened his mouth to respond, only to shut it again and give her a wrinkled brow.

Dialing up a half smile, she held a shrug. "When you're the First Lady, compromise takes on new meaning."

He grinned. "Like getting your own way?"

"Precisely."

He scratched his chin. "How about Mrs. Conklin? No more Ma'ams. I promise."

In his ear, sporting an accent, a man's voice: "Mister Special Agent Winchester."

She lifted a thumb. "I suppose I can deal with that."

Winchester raised his left wrist to his mouth. "Copy. Please identify yourself."

"Who I am is of no concern to you. All you need to know is this...at this very moment, my men are closing in on you and the First Lady."

Scowling, Winchester glanced at the woman near him then peered over the edge of the rooftop. A couple blocks away, he saw armed men on the streets, some ducking into nearby shops, others peeking through glass windows.

"All of your compadres are either deceased or incapacitated, Mister Winchester. And as you know, communications all over Panama are down, and the roadways are out. So, you have no one coming to your rescue. In time, I *will* find you and the First Lady." A moment. "Save me the trouble and show yourselves. I give you my word I will let you, and whoever is with you, go your separate way, unharmed. I only want the First Lady."

Winchester darted to another edge of the building and looked down to see more men outside the front of the four-story office building he was standing atop.

"So, what is it going to be, Mister Special Agent Winchester? Do you want to live or die?"

"Make no mistake," said the agent. "Mister Special Agent Winchester is going to live." A pulse. "Oh, and he also says," he took Caroline by the arm and hurried toward the rooftop door, "go," he cursed, "yourself."

Caroline arched her brows.

After turning off his radio, "Apologies for the language," he drew his Glock G19 then opened the door. "Stay behind me and stay close, Mrs. Conklin. We need to leave immediately. The men who ambushed us are combing the area, searching for us."

"**S**tay here," said Winchester, before he opened the door to the main stairwell. Leaning over a handrail, he saw two gunmen ascending the staircase, the pounding of their boots echoing off the concrete walls. The Secret Service man backed away, took the First Lady's hand, and rushed to the rear staircase at the opposite side of the fourth floor.

"You seem to know your way around this place pretty well," said Caroline.

"At every one of your stops, I have at least two fallback locations identified in case anything goes sideways." He opened the back stairwell door, "Wait here," then peeked over the handrail to see two more men coming up the stairs. Uttering a mental curse word, he retreated to take FLOTUS's hand.

The two hurried toward the north side of the floor. Rounding the corner at the end of a short hallway, they made a left and came to a set of metal doors.

"What are you doing?" said Caroline. "The power's out."

With a flick of his wrist, Winchester opened his black Benchmade ADAMAS G10 folding knife. He wormed the Benchmade's drop-point, 3.82-inch blade between the shiny elevator doors. "You still have that persuader I gave you?"

She lifted the two-foot-long pipe. "It's right here."

"Stick it in the gap when I," he pried apart the doors enough to get four fingers between them, "get this open enough to," dropping the knife, he employed his other four fingers and grunted while manhandling the doors, "okay, now...jam it in there."

Caroline pushed the pipe into the gap.

He claimed the metal tube, "I got it," and used it to pry open the doors a foot. Wedging his right shoulder into the space, he pushed while driving his back rearward until the doors opened another two feet.

"I still don't know how you think you're going to get this going. There's no electricity."

"We don't need electricity." Winchester stooped to snag his knife, fold it, and stow it in a pants pocket before he slid the pipe into his waistband at the small of his back. "We're going to," he covered the pipe with his jacket and sat, his legs hanging into the elevator shaft, "climb down."

"Uh," Caroline's eyes grew bigger, "pardon? It sounded like you said climb down."

He rolled onto his stomach and scooted over the edge. Grabbing the top rung of a ladder attached to the shaft's wall, he snaked his body into the shaft and got two feet on a rung a few feet below. He then looked up and raised his left arm. "Take my hand."

After leaning forward an inch to peer into the black hole below, she shook her head. "Uh-uh. No way. I can't."

"Yes, you can. One step at a time. I'll be right beneath you. You can do this."

Grimacing, she bit her lower lip while giving the darkness another quick look. "Isn't there another way?"

"We have at least four gunmen coming up the stairs from two different directions. We'd be immediately caught in a crossfire." He pumped his hand, beckoning her. "You can do this, Mrs. Conklin. I won't let you fall."

She made another screwy face, shot a glance over her shoulder, then did a nervous jig, "Oh, I don't like this," before finally sitting on her butt and sticking her legs into the shaft. "Earlier I found out I'm claustrophobic. Now," rolling to her stomach, she inched her thighs over the floor, "now I'm thinking I'm also afraid of heights."

"It is with the utmost professionalism that I do this, Mrs. Conklin." With his left hand, Winchester pushed on her butt, his palm acting like a seat. "Easy now."

Feeling his hand on her bottom, "Well, at least I'm not," the First Lady grabbed the first rung with her right hand, "not wearing a," she wriggled herself off the floor, her right toe finding a lower rung, "a skirt anyway."

He took a step down, making room for her. "That's it. You're doing great."

She got a better hold with her right foot.

"Now put your left foot right next to your right."

She followed his instructions before lowering herself into the shaft.

Winchester let go of her butt to reach around her legs

and grab the ladder with both hands. "Try to keep your," he hesitated, "your *booty* on my left shoulder as we go down."

"Bet you never thought you'd ever say *that* to the First Lady."

"Not in a million years, Ma'am—I mean, Mrs. Conklin." A beat. "We do this together, in unison. Make sure you have good handholds before you step off a rung, okay?"

Caroline nodded. "Okay."

"Handholds, step, step. Handholds, step, step. That's our rhythm. Bum-bum. Bum. Bum." A beat. "Bum-bum. Bum. Bum. Got it?"

"I think so."

Together as one, Winchester and POTUS's wife took the first two rungs downward.

In her head, Caroline was hearing the beat he had established. *Bum-bum. Bum. Bum.*

Seconds later, they passed the third floor.

His left cheek pressing against her right hip, he lifted his eyes. "Doing great, Mrs. Conklin. Doing great." His heart thumping against his chest, all he could envision was one of the gunmen poking his head into the shaft and opening fire. The first floor couldn't come soon enough.

"You know," said the First Lady, "this is sort of like dancing."

"Do you and the President enjoy dancing?"

They reached the second floor.

"Well, I do, but James not so—"

Her left foot slipped off a rung, and her body twisted and slid off Winchester's shoulder, her right foot skidding off a tick later.

He let go of the ladder with his left hand to wrap an arm around her torso and pin her to himself. "I got you."

Feeling a clamping pressure on her left breast, her legs flailing as she struggled to get a foothold, she looked down but couldn't see the elevator car. Everything just looked black.

"Don't panic. I got you. Try to get your feet under you."

She bent her right knee, slammed her high heel onto a rung, and pulled herself up to get her left foot on the same rung. A couple deep breaths later, her chest heaving, she blew air upward.

"You good?" he asked.

"I'm good. I'm good."

"All right. Let's keep going. Remember, Bum-bum. Bum. Bum."

Caroline nodded at the ladder a few inches from her nose. "Okay. I'm ready."

The two descended another nine feet.

"Hold up," said Winchester.

She stopped.

He hopped onto the car and reached up to help her the rest of the way down. "Great job, Mrs. Conklin." He took a knee and grabbed the handle to the car's access door.

It was locked.

The First Lady straightened her clothing, fixed her hair, and adjusted her left breast, a slight grimace adorning her features.

Winchester spotted her as he whipped open his Benchmade and began working on the latch, his cheeks reddening. "My apologies for getting a little handsy there."

"I won't tell if you don't."

He smiled at her quick comeback under stress. *She's a real class act.* Five seconds later, he had the access door open and was halfway through the opening. He jumped into the car, looked up, and raised both arms. "Your turn, Mrs. Conklin."

After repeating what she had done to get into the shaft, sitting, rolling, and scooting, she pushed off.

Winchester caught her and gracefully set her feet on the floor before shoving the Benchmade's blade between the closed elevator doors. Thirty seconds later, with FLOTUS's assistance and the pipe, he had the doors open enough for him to squeeze sideways through them, his Glock in hand. After clearing the nearby area, he muscled open the doors another foot, took the First Lady's left hand in his, and escorted her away from the elevator.

Operating on instinct, Winchester made a beeline for the back entrance of the building. He and the First Lady were ten yards away when he glanced over his shoulder to see a man in a Panamanian police officer's uniform raising an AK-47 rifle. Winchester pushed FLOTUS one way while going the opposite direction, gaining separation, and hopefully drawing gunfire away from her.

The klak-klak of the AK boomed.

Several 123-grain, 7.62x39mm bullets opened holes in the wall behind Winchester.

Covering her ears, Caroline Conklin let out a squeal while pivoting away from the noise.

Dropping to one knee, Winchester returned fire, felling the police imposter with five rounds. "Are you hit?"

"No." She shook her head. "It's just—no, I'm okay."

"Run for the back door."

She ran.

On her heels, he took two steps then stopped to spy a rectangular object on the dead man's belt. He faced the fleeing woman then sprinted for the dead man. "Don't go outside yet!" Squatting over the corpse, he claimed the rifle and a spare banana-shaped magazine before grabbing what had caught his eye moments ago, a walkie-talkie. He slung the rifle, stowed the other items in jacket pockets, then bolted for the First Lady while swapping magazines on his Glock, topping it off. "Stand back."

Caroline backed away from the door.

His gun up, he pushed on the horizontal bar, peeked through the gap, then cleared the area. "All right." He beckoned her. "Come on."

Together, they picked their way through the streets, dodging abandoned vehicles and debris while stomping through water puddles. Winchester kept the First Lady close, helping her navigate around parts of buildings and trash scattered along their path.

"Where are we going?" she asked.

"To my second fallback." He rounded a corner and pulled up short to gawk at the way ahead, which was still flooded. "Damn it." Backtracking, he and the First Lady, took a circuitous route around the blockage.

Seven minutes later, he led her up an incline, a wooded lane, their shoes sinking into sloppy mud. Trees on either side of them stood in bodies of water.

"Are you sure we're not headed for more problems?"

"The place we're going sits on a hill. I was here yesterday, and it was still above water."

Two minutes later, they took the lane to the left, and a two-story stone house came into view, a tall antenna rising from the roof's 'A-framed' peak. The land behind, and to the right, of the house was dry and had been cleared out to fifty yards, but many of the trees along the tree line had come down in the storm, creating a crosshatch of trunks and branches in the backyard.

Winchester pushed aside some junk the surging waters had deposited in a lower, narrower part of the lane before helping Caroline as she concentrated on her footfalls in the muck.

After ascending the rest of the lane, and passing between two wooden split-rail fences, they came to the front door of the house.

Caroline regarded all the different-sized stones fitted perfectly together. "Is anyone home?"

"Not that I'm aware of. No one in this area has been allowed to return to their homes." Winchester tried the doorknob.

It was locked.

"Wait here." He disappeared around the corner of the house.

Caroline turned her back on the front door to gander at a wood pile on the porch, a double-bit axe wedged into one of the top logs. Further away from the structure, she saw a bicycle leaning against a small shack missing half of its roof. Pivoting her head to the left, she glimpsed more junk the water and winds had strewn around.

Behind her, the door opened.

She whirled around to see Winchester. "How'd you get in?"

"The back door was open."

She stepped into the house. "Was it truly open or did

you," a beat, "*persuade* it to open?"

He closed the front door. "No. It was actually unlocked. In their hurry to leave, they must've forgotten. Not that that would've done much good. When looters want in, they'll get in. I'll be right back." Taking the steps two at a time, he scaled a staircase near a stone fireplace.

Caroline made a visual pass around the home's interior to see the usual pieces in a living room—two couches, coffee table, end tables, small television, easy chair. Underfoot, tightly woven brown carpeting met up with dark-brown paneling on the walls. *Nice, but it's awfully dark in here. Could use a—*

Heavy footfalls came from overhead.

She looked up to see Winchester peering over a wooden handrail.

"Up here, Mrs. Conklin."

She climbed the carpeted staircase while gliding her left hand along the handrail. "You seem to be searching for something."

"You saw that tall antenna outside, didn't you?"

"I did."

He led her into the first room on the right, a room set up like a mini communications center.

Caroline ogled a wide wooden desk on the far side of the space. The desk went from the wall on the left to the one on the right. It was littered with mechanical equipment. Some of it looked familiar to her, especially one device, the one centered on the desk.

After switching on the commandeered walkie talkie, setting the volume to low, and placing it on the desk, off to his left, Winchester examined the large radio in front of him, taking a few moments to familiarize himself with the controls while listening to the chatter coming from the walkie talkie. His Spanish was rusty, but he picked up on enough words to fill in the blanks on the rest.

FLOTUS wagged a finger at the main attraction, the bulky device taking center stage on the desk. "My dad had one of those. That's a ham radio."

"Yes, it is."

"He used to talk to people from all over the world." She dialed up a thin grin. "I used to sit on his knee and listen to him say all these cool things."

Winchester looked under the desk then sidestepped left to open and close cabinet doors.

"One time," she continued, "he was talking to someone from France. He knew some of the language, so he and whoever he was talking to were having a conversation in French."

Winchester opened a door and smiled at three 100 amp-hour 12-volt LiFePO4 batteries. "Bingo."

Lost in happy memories, she stared at the equipment. "Those were good times with my father." She blinked twice then spied Winchester. "Too bad the power's out. Or, we could..."

He rotated a dial, and the radio came to life.

"...call for," she frowned at him, "what the...is the

power back on?"

"It *is* for us." He sat in front of the radio and started flipping switches and adjusting dials. "There are a few backup batteries," he paused to thrust out an index finger to his left, "down in that cabinet there," before returning to his work. "Plenty of juice for what we need to do."

The First Lady put her right hand on the back of his chair and her left palm on the desk, leaning forward to squint at everything on the furniture's surface. "This guy has quite the setup. My dad didn't have this much stuff."

"Yeah. Puts mine to shame, too."

She spied him. "You have a ham radio?"

"Just got my license a few months ago. I guess you could say I'm an old-school kind of guy. I prefer fishing to video games; tinkering in the workshop to surfing the Internet; and talking over the radio to," he half shook his head before bouncing a shoulder, "to face-gabbing or chatting or whatever the heck it's called now." A tick. "So far, I," he worked knobs, "I haven't had much time to dig deep into the ham radio."

"Well, I suppose if your," she faced the radio, "slave-driving boss wasn't flitting off to other countries, you could spend more time with your hobbies."

Winchester lifted a corner of his mouth while he physically searched frequencies. "I'm *exactly* where I need to be, Mrs. Conklin."

"Believe me." Recalling the last hour's events, she patted him twice on his left shoulder. "I'm extremely happy you're here."

He switched among frequencies and ran the needle back and forth over the dial.

The speaker squawked, but nothing intelligible filled the room.

After repeated attempts at reaching the tower at the airport, another nearby ham operator, or even one of the three Sikorsky VH-60N White Hawk helicopters that had been flown in on a C-17 Globemaster III five days earlier—so the First Lady could survey the damage to Panama from the air—Winchester glimpsed his watch. 6:22. He peeked out the window at the encroaching nightfall. *Fifteen minutes to sunset.* His goal of not spending the night in the field with the First Lady was not looking attainable. And his gut told him the guy he told to go 'bleep' off was determined to find her at all costs.

Sensing his frustration, Caroline motioned toward the walkie talkie. "What about that? Will that work to reach your team?"

He shook his head. "The range isn't long enough. I grabbed that to keep tabs on enemy troop movements. If we're forced to bugout, I want a head start."

She made a one-eighty and perched on the lip of the desk. A moment later, she crossed her ankles and folded her forearms over her belly.

Slumping deeper into the chair, he scowled at the ham radio.

"Won't the agents at the airport eventually realize we're overdue and send someone out?" asked Caroline.

Winchester scratched his chin. "Eventually, yes, but I'm not sure we have the luxury of *eventually.*" He gestured at the walkie. "These guys know the area and are conducting a coordinated block-by-block search. With so many roads unpassable, I'm not confident we could slip through their forces undetected. And even if reinforcements left right now, they're still an hour," he cocked his head at a series of numbers below what appeared to be the ham operator's call sign, "away."

Caroline heard the hitch in his voice and turned to spy his wrinkle brow. "What is it?"

Winchester verified the ham radio had the autopatch feature. *Could it really be that easy?* He ran through the channels. After thirty seconds, he picked up an ongoing contact and broke into the conversation. "This is," he eyed the radio's console to see this station's call sign, "this is Foxtrot Foxtrot Zulu Six, requesting an emergency autopatch. I repeat, this is Foxtrot Foxtrot Zulu Six, requesting an emergency autopatch. Over."

"Foxtrot Foxtrot Zulu Six, this is Alpha Yankee Four Kilo. You're clear for autopatch. Over."

"Roger that, Alpha," he scribbled AY4K on a scratch pad while repeating the station's call sign, "Yankee Four Kilo. Switching to autopatch. Over." Winchester held down the microphone button, pressed the activation sequence of tones, then released the microphone button.

Five seconds went by, and no acknowledging transmission came through.

He repeated the steps again and waited.

Nothing.

He held his arms out at ten and two o'clock, palms up. *What am I doing wrong?* After trying one more time and getting the same silence, *Maybe the signal's not strong enough,* he hit the microphone. "Alpha Yankee Four Kilo, this is Foxtrot Foxtrot Zulu Six. Are you there? Over."

"Foxtrot Foxtrot Zulu Six, Alpha Yankee Four Kilo is standing by. Over."

"Having difficulty accessing autopatch. Are you able to assist? Over."

"Affirmative, Foxtrot Foxtrot Zulu Six. Switching to autopatch. Over."

Seconds later, a dial tone came through the speaker.

Winchester pressed the tone keys for the cell phone number for one of the Secret Service agents guarding the helicopters at Tocumen International Airport in Panama City.

Moments later, through the ham radio's speaker, a man's voice: "Agent Wilcox."

"This is Special Agent Winchester of the Secret Service calling via amateur radio. This is not a secure line. Do you copy? Over." Winchester let up on the microphone button.

"Copy that, Agent Winchester. What's going on down there? We've been unable to establish communications with your detail. Is everything okay?"

Winchester waited a couple seconds then depressed the microphone button. "FLOTUS motorcade attacked. Sunflower unharmed and with me. I repeat, Sunflower is unharmed. Status of detail is unknown. Requesting immediate extraction. Hostiles closing in. Over."

Wilcox let loose with a string of mild expletives. "Copy that. We're rolling. ETA in," a beat, "sixty-two minutes."

Winchester mashed the mic button. "Negative. Negative. Not good enough. We'll be overrun before then. Requesting airlift. Over."

Five seconds passed.

"Copy that," said Wilcox. "Air support is winding up as we speak. What's your location?"

Using a map of the area, one he had downloaded to his cell phone prior to the start of the First Lady's trip, Winchester provided his coordinates then said, "The area north of the structure is dry with enough room for a set-down or a hover rescue. Over."

"Copy. New ETA in," said Wilcox before pausing a beat, "twenty-two minutes. Hang in there, Remi. We're coming."

"Copy that," replied Winchester. "Over and out." He let go of the mic button, waited two seconds, then hit it again while referring to his notes. "Alpha Yankee Four Kilo, this is," he glanced up at the call sign placard for this station, "Foxtrot Foxtrot Zulu Six. Do you read me? Over."

"Reading you loud and clear, Foxtrot Foxtrot Zulu Six."

"Thanks for the assist," said Winchester. "You may have *literally* just saved lives. Over."

"Glad I could help, Agent Winchester. Over."

"By the way, who am I speaking to? Over."

"This is retired Major Stanley Jensen, United States Army, living out my golden years in beautiful Panama.

Over."

Winchester let a grin come and go. "Don't be too hard on yourself, Major. Not everyone has what it takes to be a Navy man. Lieutenant, here. Seventh fleet. Over."

"I'd tell you what I think of you Navy men, Lieutenant..."

Winchester heard a smile in the man's voice.

"...but I suspect you have one of our nation's treasures there with you. So..."

Winchester glimpsed the First Lady.

She half grinned at him.

"...I'll keep things clean and," continued Major Jensen, "say this...if you ever find yourself in Panama in the future, I'd be willing to cross over the line and buy a Navy man a beer. Over."

"And this Navy man might just take you up on that offer, Major. Much obliged for the help. Over."

"I'll be standing by in case you need further assistance. Give my best to Sunflower, and I'll be praying for a speedy extraction. Over."

"Will do and thank you, Major. Foxtrot Foxtrot Zulu Six signing off." Winchester released the microphone button and faced FLOTUS. "Major Stanley Jensen, US Army, sends his regards."

She smiled at the radio. "He seems like a nice man."

Winchester checked his watch. "Twenty-one minutes until the air cavalry gets here." He spied the walkie and listened for a beat. Based on what he was hearing, the men were still clearing buildings in town. So far, no one had thought to check the homes on the perimeter. Perhaps they thought the area was too flooded for anyone to reach. Or maybe their plan was to close the noose by clearing the town then working their way outward. He eyeballed his watch again. *Twenty minutes.*

"I must say," said Caroline, a slight smile on her face. "Watching you," she motioned toward the radio, "work that thing, I couldn't help but think you reminded me a lot of my father," she showed Winchester her palms and quickly followed up with, "when he was *your* age that is, and I was a little kid of course."

Winchester nodded.

She half closed an eye at him. "You handled yourself very professionally over the radio waves. Seems like you have a knack for this." She bobbed her head from side to side. "As well as keeping First Ladies alive."

He stood. "That's my *only* priority, Mrs. Conklin, getting you back to your family." He inspected the AK-47, making sure there was a round in the chamber and a full magazine in the magwell, before leaning the weapon against the wall.

"So, you were in the Navy," said Caroline.

"I was. I spent four years there before I—"

Male voice: "Mister Special Agent Winchester."

Winchester and the First Lady whipped their heads toward the walkie talkie.

Three seconds passed.

"I know you're listening in on our communications. Clever move, taking the walkie talkie. Very clever."

Winchester strolled up to the walkie.

"I know you told me to go," the male voice cursed, "myself during our last conversation; however, I wanted to extend one last chance at saving yourself. Show yourselves now, and I'll let you and your compadres go without repercussions. As I said before, I only want the First Lady."

Caroline's eyes grew bigger as she went from the walkie to the special agent to the walkie again.

"You have my word. No harm will come to you."

Winchester raised the walkie and depressed a switch. "I wish I could extend the same courtesy, but if we cross paths, I *will* kill you."

Laughter came through the device's speaker. "It's only a matter of time, Mister Special Agent Winchester. There are only so many places you can hide. I will find you. And when I do," a beat, "it will not go so well for you, my friend."

Caroline held out her hand.

Winchester frowned at her.

"Give it to me."

"Nothing good can come from indulging him, Mrs. Conklin."

She wiggled her fingers.

He relented. "Push this to talk."

She pushed the switch he had pointed out to her.

"Listen here, you pathetic little man. I know your type. I've been dealing with cockroaches like you my whole life. You compensate for your penile shortcomings by..."

Winchester raised an eyebrow.

"...belittling everyone around you. Well, just so you know, I'm not afraid of you," she glimpsed the man a foot away from her, "and neither is Agent Winchester. You murdered innocent people, and you will pay for your crimes. So, bring it on." She let off the switch then quickly thumbed it again while bringing the walkie to her mouth. "And go *screw* yourself." After releasing the switch, she turned the walkie over in her hands. "How do you turn this off? I don't want to hear his smug, despicable voice anymore."

Winchester claimed the communication device, turned it off, then set it on the desk. It was useless now, anyway. Even if the enemy stayed on the same channel, he couldn't trust the information coming from it.

FLOTUS took a deep breath, exhaled, then pushed a lock of hair away from her face. She looked up to see Winchester staring at her. One corner of his mouth was curled upward a fraction of an inch. "I'm sorry," she said.

"Don't be."

"I just get so upset at men like that. They're so annoying with their," she made fists, "with their threats and their," she shook her fists, "ooh, I just wanted to *punch* him in the face."

Winchester couldn't stop his grin from growing

wider.

She took another breath, smoothed her clothes, then faced him. "Please don't mention any of this to my husband. He's always telling me I need to be more diplomatic."

"I won't tell if you don't."

Hearing his words—her words from earlier—she regarded her protector then let out a quick chuckle.

He winked at her. He didn't know if it was appropriate to wink at the First Lady, but he couldn't stop himself. Recalling Major Stanley Jensen's words, *I suspect you have one of our nation's treasures there with you,* Winchester nodded. *She's a national treasure, all right.*

6:35 P.M.

Winchester checked his watch then stared out the upstairs window that faced the front of the house where the driveway was being swallowed up by the encroaching darkness. Sunset was two minutes away, and help was, by his estimate, almost five minutes away. He pictured the backyard and saw a hasty extraction. *Daylight or night-time, a loud, thumping helicopter is going to carry far and wide and draw the attention of anyone and everyone in the area. A beat. This is going to have to be a fast evac.*

Caroline sauntered up to him to stare out the window.

He made sure his earpiece was securely in his ear then tuned the radio on his belt to the backup channel his fellow agents would be using when they arrived.

"After everything we've gone through," said the First Lady, "the shooting; climbing down the elevator shaft; ducking and dodging those men to get here..."

He looked up, took her by the elbow, and gently pushed. "Please step away from the window, Mrs. Conklin."

She followed his guidance and backed away from the

pane. "I thought they wanted to kidnap me, not *kill* me."

"I'm not taking any chances." He poked his chin at her. "You were saying?"

She glimpsed him. "What?" A beat. "Oh, right. After everything we've been through," her body gave off an involuntary shudder, "I've never been more afraid than I am right now, *waiting* for help to arrive. I keep thinking something bad is going to happen, and I'll never see my daughter and husband again." A moment later, she faced him then dipped her chin to gape at the floor. "I sound ridiculous, don't I?"

After half closing one eye at her, he glanced out the window then came back to her. "I've loved the water ever since I can remember. When I was six, my dad taught me how to swim in the lake near our cabin in Minnesota. I loved that summer." A thin grin formed on the storyteller's face. "It was the best time I ever had with him. I can still feel those cool waters and his strong arms holding me as I flopped around," he chuckled, "thinking I was actually swimming."

Caroline half smiled.

"Anyway, a month later, when it came time to head home, I had become a pretty good swimmer. At least that's what Dad had told me."

She nodded. "That's what good parents do. They see the best in their kids, build them up."

He agreed before his features turned sour. "A year later, he was diagnosed with pancreatic cancer and was gone before Christmas."

"Oh," Caroline reached out to lay a hand on his arm, "I'm so sorry. And you were so young."

"Turned seven three days after he passed."

The First Lady pursed her lips, fighting to hold back the moisture gathering behind her eyes. "You poor thing."

Winchester stiffened his spine and exhaled. "Fast forward a decade and his hard work paid off. I won a conference title in high school swimming and came within a few hundredths of a second of taking a state championship."

"I'm sure your father knows and is proud of you."

He nodded. "After I left the Navy, I bounced around a bit and finally settled in a town off the coast of Northern California. I bought a surf ski and got pretty good at it. Knifing through the waters on the open ocean, a wind at my back, my muscles feeling the burn," he shut his eyes and filled his lungs, "there's nothing more exhilarating...at least not for me."

Caroline shifted her weight from one foot to the other, her attention squarely on the Secret Service agent. She sensed this was building up to something, since he didn't seem the kind of man akin to sharing his feelings with relative strangers.

"One weekend, I wanted to get a quick run in. I had some errands I needed to take care of, but I had some time. The skies were overcast, but the weatherman said there wasn't any rain in the forecast. So, I took the surf ski out," he paused, "I don't remember how many miles I was out at sea. But the waters were calm, and there was a nice wind. I was hitting a good stride, a good pace. Then, all of a sudden, a rogue wave came out of nowhere."

Caroline's eyes bulged.

"I worked the pedals on the rudder, trying to steer into the wave and ride it upward." Winchester shook his head. "There wasn't enough time. It hit me square on the starboard side and drove me downward. The force was so great that it yanked the leg leash off my ankle. When I surfaced, the waters were calm again, but my surf ski was long gone."

"But you had a life jacket on, though, right?"

He shook his head. "I was wearing a buoyancy aid. It helps you stay up while you're treading water, but you can't just relax and float." He held a shrug. "Who can predict once-in-a-hundred-years rogue waves? Normally, buoyancy aids are fine when your surf ski is attached to your leg."

"What did you do?"

"Every direction I looked, I only saw water and overcast skies. Visibility was not great, so I couldn't make out land. I know I wasn't that far from the coast. I'm a strong swimmer. I could've swum to shore. But not knowing which direction shore was, I could've very well started swimming further out to sea."

"You're killing me here, Remi. I mean, I know you

obviously survived, but how?”

“I treaded water for six hours before a yacht happened by just before the sun went down. I screamed my head off, a bright light from the boat found me, and they motored over and tossed me a line.”

Caroline let out the air she had been holding, her shoulders slumping a bit.

“The reason I’m telling you this story is that,” he bit his lower lip for a moment, “all the while I was treading water, I wasn’t afraid. I was calm. I kept thinking about what I could do to help my situation, kept looking for watercraft, driftwood, anything that could improve my chances of surviving.” He chuckled under his breath. “And I prayed.” He shook his head. “Boy, did I pray. Jesus and I became best buds that day.”

FLOTUS smiled.

Winchester faced Caroline. “But when that yacht found me, those were the longest, most terrifying ten, fifteen minutes of my life. I kept thinking I was going to get a cramp, lose what little strength I had left and sink beneath the waves, or that a shark was going to come up and bite me in half.”

She frowned at him.

He pointed out the window. “That helicopter is only minutes away, Mrs. Conklin. Don’t give in to the devil. He feeds off our fear, loves to whisper to us...you screwed up; you’re not good enough; she’s out of your league; you’re ugly; you’re fat; you’ll never get that promotion;

give up; or," Winchester focused on the First Lady, "you'll never see your family again." He shook his head. "That fear is a lie. Don't believe it."

Caroline cocked her head at him.

"Just like when I was treading water, thinking about how I could help myself, *you* need to do the same thing. Focus on what gives you strength—your daughter, and your husband. You *will* see them again. I promise you. With every fiber of my being, I'm going to make damn sure you get on that helicopter and back to your family. You hear me?"

She swallowed hard then nodded before swiping a tear from under her right eye. "You remind me of a man I've recently gotten to know quite well. When my daughter Abigail was kidnapped, this man looked me square in the eye and told me he was going to find her and bring her home." Caroline half shook her head. "With every law enforcement agency in the country searching for my Abby, I'll be danged if *he* wasn't the one to," a beat, "find her and bring her home to me...just like he said he would."

Winchester scowled at the First Lady. "You're talking about Aaron Hardy."

She faced her protector. "You *know* him?"

"We've never met, but I've heard the talk that he seems to have the President's ear. In fact, from what I'm told, he's the only person—outside of us agents—who's allowed to see your husband behind closed doors without first being disarmed."

"Well, I can't speak to any of that, but Aaron has definitely become a very dear friend of James' and mine." Caroline huffed out a quick chuckle. "And Abby, too, for that matter. She's taken a real shine to him." FLOTUS blinked a few times then faced Winchester. "Anyway, I mention him, because I sense the two of you share a common trait."

Winchester arched his brows.

"You both have that hardened, determined, I-will-not-fail attitude."

He lifted a corner of his mouth at the high praise. "Thank you, Mrs. Conklin."

"You're welcome. And by the way," a beat, "when you get me on that helicopter," she half closed an eye while poking a finger at him, "you *damn* well better be there, too. We're getting out of this together. Got it?"

"From your lips to the Almighty's ears."

"I get the feeling you're a praying man. Am I right?"

He scratched his chin while peering out the window. "When I was young, Mom made my sisters and me go to church with her. *Every* Sunday. But I wasn't interested. I had other things, *better* things to do. Sure, I *went*. Had to. Mom made us. But when I turned eighteen and joined the Navy," he shook his head, "God was the furthest thing from my mind." He faced Caroline. "That surf ski incident, however, got me thinking about Him in a whole new way. As I said, Jesus and me," Winchester held up two overlapped fingers, "we were tight that day.

"In fact," continued Winchester, "I've often wondered if God *sent* that rogue wave," he huffed, "to sort of knock me off my game and get my attention."

The First Lady smiled. "He does that from time to time."

"Oh," Winchester arched his eyebrows and nodded, "don't I know it. Over the last few years, I've also speculated that at no point was I ever in any *real* danger. He knew *exactly* how long I could tread water. He made sure that yacht took the course it took. And He kept all the creatures of the deep away from me." A pulse. "I believe God simply wanted to spend some alone time with me, talk to me." Winchester rolled his eyes upward. "Well, it worked. I've been listening and talking to Him ever since."

The agent met Caroline's gaze. "So, to answer your question, Mrs. Conklin...yes, I'm a praying man."

"In that case," she held out her right hand, "would you mind praying with me? I think it would help me focus on something other than," she paused while recalling his words from earlier, "the things the devil wants to whisper to me."

He took her hand in his. "Of course. I'd be honored."

A minute later, after the First Lady had finished her prayer, she gave him a light squeeze, "Amen," then let go of his hand.

"Amen," he said.

"Thank you, Remi. I think..."

Winchester's earpiece crackled.

"...that really helped soothe my nerves."

In his ear, a male voice: "Winchester, this is Wilcox. Do you copy? Over."

Winchester brought his left wrist to his mouth. "This is Winchester. How far away are you? Over." He cocked his head, his ears picking up a faint thumping noise coming out of the west.

"We're one minute out. I repeat, we're one minute out. Over."

"Copy that." He took the First Lady by the arm, and the two made their way out of the room and down the stairs. "Sunflower on the move. Rendezvous: north side of structure. Be advised. Hostiles nearby. Possible hot extraction. Over."

"Copy. See you in sixty, Remi. Over."

Winchester escorted the First Lady through the house, out the back door, and into a backyard that was quickly being overtaken by the black of night.

The sound of helicopter blades slicing through the air was growing louder by the second.

Keeping Caroline close to him, the AK-47 in his right hand, he steadied her as she stepped over and around scattered debris and branches on their way toward the open space on the lawn. Further out, multiple downed trees encircled them. The twosome stopped to look up, over their left shoulders.

The dark-green underbelly of the Sikorsky VH-60N "White Hawk" helicopter came into view above the treetops. The aircraft was smaller than the President's VH-3D Sea King. But it was also newer than the Sea King. The White Hawk hovered above the open area before slowly descending.

"Come on," said Winchester, escorting the First Lady to the southwest, pulling up short of a downed tree.

Overhead, two more White Hawks floated above the trees.

Two minutes later, the 65-foot-long Sikorsky touched down.

Five men in black suits poured out of the cabin and ran toward Winchester and the First Lady.

"Keep your head down," said Winchester, taking her by the elbow as the two darted to meet the oncoming Secret Service agents. "You're almost home, Mrs. Conk—"

Rifle fire erupted from their four o'clock.

"Down, down!" He pushed her to the wet grass, spun to face the house, then took a knee while shouldering the AK.

Flashes of light came from different points near the house.

Hearing pistol rounds going off behind him, the rounds coming from his fellow agents, he raised his rifle and zeroed in on the flashes ahead of him; specifically, the barely visible silhouettes beyond them. He laid down a steady stream of automatic fire while swinging the gun from left to right and back again.

The rifle ran dry.

Pivoting, Winchester yanked out the empty magazine while shouting at the approaching agents. "Take her. I'll cover your retreat."

Two men wrapped their arms around Caroline, hoisted her off the ground, and ran.

"No," she screamed, looking back at Winchester. "You promised me."

"I'm," he jammed his only spare mag into the long gun, "I'm right behind you, Ma'am." After chambering a round and switching the AK to semi-auto, he turned his back on her and carefully picked out his targets, working the trigger once every second.

"Remi," yelled Caroline. "Remi!"

Her voice trailing off behind him, he concentrated on the silhouettes and squeezed off precision shots.

Two silhouettes, and their accompanying flashes, disappeared.

Pistol fire on his right made him look that way.

Wilcox was down on one knee, his Glock in both hands, firing away at the silhouettes. The man spotted Winchester out of the corner of his eye. "You didn't think I was going to leave my Lieutenant high and dry, did you?"

Winchester half grinned at the dark-haired man, two years his senior, who had been under his command when the two had been stationed with the US Navy's seventh fleet. A tick later, he resumed his covering fire.

Together, the men either kept the enemy's heads down or outright 'took off' the enemy's heads.

Winchester stole a glance over his shoulder to see the First Lady being pushed into the Sikorsky. He tapped Wilcox on the left shoulder. "Go. I'll cover you."

Standing, Wilcox backpedaled toward the aircraft while firing.

His Glock's slide locked open.

"Reloading."

Winchester rose to his feet and made a steady, calculated retreat, easing off one shot for every two rearward steps he took.

Wilcox slammed a fresh magazine into his gun and thumbed the slide forward. "Up and running. Let's go. Let's go."

The AK ran dry again.

Winchester dropped the rifle, drew his Glock 19, and continued shooting at silhouettes. Hearing a grunt, he cranked his head around to see Wilcox doubled over and holding himself. He darted to his friend's side. "Where?"

"Stomach." Wilcox grimaced. "Damn it."

Winchester draped his buddy's right arm around his neck, and the two hurried as fast as they could toward the White Hawk, looking like they were failing miserably in the three-legged race at the company's annual picnic.

Bullets whizzed by them.

His left arm hugging his 'race partner,' Winchester let go of Wilcox's right arm to let loose with a few blind shots behind him.

Fifty feet from the helo, a burning sensation shot up the back of Winchester's right thigh.

He stumbled before both men toppled to the grass as one. Lifting his head to see an agent exiting the chopper, he thrust out his left index finger and bellowed, "Get her in the air...*now.*"

The Secret Service agent obeyed.

Seconds later, the White Hawk was rising off the grass.

Winchester rolled to his back and emptied his pistol at his adversaries before reloading and repeating the process. "Hold on, Cox."

"Easy for you to say," said Wilcox. "You're not the one with a bullet in your—"

A projectile tore through Wilcox's upper arm, cutting him off in mid-sentence.

...

The rising Sikorsky cleared the trees and banked left, away from the gunfight below. On her stomach, on the floor of the helicopter, determined she wasn't going to be held down this time, FLOTUS wrangled free of the man on top of her and managed to get a quick look outside the aircraft.

A hundred feet below, Winchester lay on his back, legs splayed, his firearm in both hands and aimed toward the house. Flashes of light came from the house.

At the last moment, Caroline saw him reach up and clutch his upper chest. A tick later, she saw him tip his head backward, a split-second before his upper body collapsed onto the grass. "No," she shrieked before confronting the men around her. "Go back. You have to go back for him." She pointed. "He's hurt." Her voice cracked. "He needs you."

"We're sorry, Ma'am," said the man who was now lifting himself off her. "Your safety is our only priority." He spied the back of the pilot's helmet and raised his voice. "Get us out of here."

The pilot made a wide turn to port, aiming to steer clear of any potential incoming rounds, then set off on a northwesterly course. A beat later, he keyed his mic. "Tocumen tower, this is White Hawk One. Do you copy? Over."

A voice inside the pilot's earmuffs: "Reading you loud and clear, White Hawk One."

"Be advised, Tocumen. We are switching call signs. White Hawk One is now going by," he glimpsed the First Lady over his left shoulder then faced forward, "Executive One Foxtrot. We're requesting clearance to land on," the pilot relayed where he wanted to set down at the airport.

"Roger that, Executive One Foxtrot. You're cleared to land. Will you be requiring assistance?"

"That's a negative, Tocumen. Just keep the skies clear.

Over."

Caroline listened to the pilot's half of the conversation, a knot of guilt welling up inside her gut. Envisioning Winchester falling onto his back, her real vision now obscured by the tears gathering at the corners of her eyes, she hung her head and cried into the floorboards.

CHAPTER 8
At Ease

Dressed in knee-high, high-heeled black boots, dark-brown, skin-tight leather pants, and a black leather jacket—oversized black sunglasses and a wide-brimmed floppy hat covering most of her face—a woman stepped out of a Cadillac sedan, a man in a black suit holding open the right-rear door for her. She hurried toward the underground shipping & receiving area's elevator, four other 'Men in Black' surrounding her.

Once inside the car, the entourage changed elevators on the first floor then proceeded to the third floor. When the doors opened, she was quickly escorted down a mostly evacuated hallway. The only people in sight were a woman in scrubs, sitting behind a desk, and a few onlookers peeking over the shoulders of a couple more wide-bodied MIBs, their arms out at their sides while they faced the gawkers.

"It's right here, Ma'am," said the nearest MIB while jogging ahead to push open a wide wooden door.

She ducked into the room.

He closed the door behind her, folded his hands in

front of his belt buckle, and turned his back to face the hallway. A second MIB took a position opposite the door from him.

• • •

Reclining in a hospital bed, wearing a gray gown, covers pulled up to his waist, a man rolled his head to his right then scurried to push himself into a more upright position when he saw who his visitor was.

"Oh, stop," said Caroline Conklin as she skittered across the room to push him back to a relaxed position. "At ease. I think you've earned some down time, don't you?"

Special Agent Remington Winchester half smiled at her before filling his lungs. "I'm surp—" he coughed into his hand for a good five or six seconds before finishing his breath and exhaling. "I'm surprised to see you, Ma'am." He couldn't help himself from giving her outfit more scrutiny, his attention ending at the large gold hoop earrings dangling from her earlobes.

She noticed. "It's not my usual look, I know, but I," removing her hat and oversized sunglasses, she slid a straight-back chair closer, sat on his two o'clock, and crossed her legs at the knee, laying the hat and sunglasses on her lap a tick later, "but I didn't want to be recognized." She lifted a hand and glanced around, her mind envisioning how the Secret Service had cleared this area of the hospital ahead of her visit. "My coming here has caused enough disruption as it is." The First Lady bounced her top leg a bit while studying him for a few moments. "You had me thinking you were dead. You know that?"

Back in Panama, once the First Lady's helicopter had left the scene, a second Sikorsky had swooped down and landed. Secret Service agents had then battled their way to the injured Winchester and Wilcox, snatched them, then made a hasty retreat to the waiting aircraft. While Wilcox's abdominal wound was serious, doctors had acted quickly to save his life. He was expected to make a complete recovery.

Fast forward to the present, Winchester now mentally reviewed his injuries, a bullet wound in his right thigh and another in his right shoulder area. The second one had been more critical, with the bullet having tumbled upon entry, coming close to hitting his right lung. "Just a couple flesh wounds," he said while making a face. "Nothing serious."

She raised an eyebrow. "Nothing serious, huh? You've had two surgeries and are only just now recovering from a nasty infection from," she pointed at his chest, "your *flesh wound* there." A beat. "And judging from that cough, you still have a touch of pneumonia still hanging around."

"I didn't know you were a doctor, Ma'am."

"We've been over this, Remi. Enough with the

Ma'ams."

"I thought that only applied to that specific moment in time." He half closed an eye at her. "And if I may, how do you know so much about my medical condition?"

"Your doctor's been keeping me informed of your progress. In fact, the nurses here say you have quite the sense of humor," she gave him a wry grin, "in addition to being a first-class flirt."

Unsure if it was the long-haired blonde or the long-legged brunette that had 'squealed' on him, maybe both, he felt his cheeks flushing as he struggled to remember which jokes he had told the two nurses. There were several light-hearted icebreakers he always had 'in the holster' for whenever he crossed paths with an attractive woman.

"I can see the flirt in you," said the First Lady, "but I didn't have you pegged as a jokester."

"Isn't there some rule that doctors and hospitals are only allowed to give out a patient's medical information to family members?"

Caroline held a half shrug. "Your doctor and I came to an agreement."

Winchester lifted a corner of his mouth. "The kind of agreement where *you* get what *you* want?"

Smiling, she wagged a finger at him. "You're catching on to how this works, Agent Winchester."

He couldn't hold back a snicker. Halfway through, he went into another coughing jag, afterwards holding a flat

     EXECUTIVE ONE FOXTROT

hand to his chest while taking as big a breath as he could, his eyes aimed at the white ceiling tiles.

FLOTUS stood, grabbed his waterglass, and held it out to him. "Here. Take a drink."

He shook his head. "I'm good."

She shook her head right back at him. "No. You're not hearing me. I took orders from you when we were dodging bullets. Now *you're* taking orders from *me*." She took his hand and wrapped it around the cup. "Don't make me treat you like a little kid and hold it up to your lips."

Winchester huffed, downed a couple sips, then forfeited the vessel. After swallowing, he gave her an overly polite smile.

She pointed at him while setting the cup on his side table. "That's the same look my daughter gives me whenever I make her do something she doesn't want to do. Good to know your maturity is on par with that of a rebellious teenager."

His shoulders shaking, he stifled a laugh while putting a hand on his chest in hopes of quelling another coughing spell. "With all due respect, Mrs. Conklin, please don't make me laugh. I feel as if I've already hacked up one lung. I'd like to keep the second one if I could." In the next instant, he regarded her. "You've really been keeping tabs on me while I've been in here?"

Caroline moved her hat and sunglasses to the edge of his side table and sat, crossing her legs at the knee once more. "I informed your doctor that he was to give me updates on your condition twice a day. And in between those times, if anything serious happened, I was to be notified as soon as possible."

"Huh." Winchester scratched his chin.

"So, I know that the wound in your leg, while painful, was indeed a somewhat minor injury. If you stay on top of your physical therapy," she leveled a finger at him, "which I *know* you will, right?"

He crossed his heart with one finger.

She nodded, "Good answer," before continuing. "If you stay on top of your therapy, you'll be up and around in no time." A tick. "But your chest wound, however, was more serious. Had the bullet gone a little more toward your sternum, it would have destroyed your lung. As it was, the bullet was most likely the cause of your infection and subsequent case of pneumonia. Your doctor did a bang-up job at treating both, and now you're well on your way to a full recovery in four to six weeks."

"I'm shooting for Four," said Winchester.

"While I'd love to have you leading my security detail in four weeks, let's make sure we don't push it, shall we?"

His brows came together as he squared shoulders with her.

"I want you at a hundred percent."

"Excuse me, Ma—Mrs. Conklin."

She half grinned at his near faux pas.

"Did you just say," he paused, "*leading* your security

detail?"

"Why," she cocked her head and touched a fore finger to her chin, "why I believe I did, yes."

He puckered his lips while his frown deepened. "While I'm honored, I'm not sure that's how the Secret Service works. They don't give a newbie like me the responsibility of keeping POTUS's wife safe."

Caroline agreed with him. "I understand that. But who better to protect me than the man who's already done exactly that? There's no better person for the task. You're perfectly qualified." A pulse. "And if the Secret Service doesn't see it that way, why I guess I'll just have to have a talk with whoever's in charge over there. He and I can come to some sort of," she winked at Winchester, "*compromise*, I'm sure."

Winchester smiled then broke out into laughter. The hacking came on as his amusement ramped up. He rolled sideways and grabbed the bed's handrail.

The First Lady stood to hand him his cup of water.

This time, he drank without being coerced. "Thank you."

"Well," she returned his cup to the side table, "I should probably get going. You need your rest." Caroline glimpsed her watch then faced him. "I would've been here earlier in the week, but I knew my presence was going to cause a stir. And you didn't need the drama when you were fighting to get better." A pulse. "But when the doctor told me you were on the mend, I figured this was the best time for me to check in on you," she toyed with the gold cross attached to the bracelet around her right wrist, "to let you know that you've been on my mind and in my prayers."

"Thank you. I appreciate that."

She regarded the patient for a good twenty seconds, her mind racing with snippets from their shared ordeal.

Winchester squirmed under the bedcovers. He was okay with silence. He just preferred being the one dishing it out.

"I'm not entirely sure if this is against Secret Service protocol, but," she leaned over his bed's handrail, gave him a gentle hug, making sure not to get anywhere near his shoulder wound, then kissed his cheek and stood upright, "but right now I really don't care." She sandwiched his right hand between hers and patted it. "From the bottom of my heart, Remi, thank you for keeping your promise, for getting me home to my family. I will be forever grateful."

"It was my duty and honor to do so," he cleared his throat then drew his lips into his mouth before squeezing her hand a bit, "Caroline."

A broad, beaming smile graced her features. "And on that happy note, I'll take my leave." She donned her hat and sunglasses, strolled to the door, then spun back, her left hand on the door handle, her right index finger aimed at the prone man. "Do what the doctor tells you to do. You hear me?"

Winchester nodded.

She poked her finger at him again. "Keep up with your therapy."

Another nod. "I promise."

"And most of all," FLOTUS paused, a twinkle in her eye, "stop flirting with the nurses. You're in here to rest, not to," she twirled an index finger at his lower half, "not to get yourself all worked up."

He gave her an up-turned thumb. "I'll try my best."

"Yeah, uh-huh," grinning, "sure you will," the First Lady of the United States pulled open the door and left the room.

— Thank You —

Thank you for purchasing and reading *Executive One Foxtrot*. I hope you enjoyed this fast-paced action thriller. And since you love patriotic action, keep reading for a sneak peek at *The Unsanctioned Patriot*, the first book in the Aaron Hardy series. Yes, that's the same Aaron Hardy that Winchester and FLOTUS talked about in this story.

All right. I'll be back soon with a new novel. Until then...

Blessings and Peace,

Alex

P.S. Don't forget your FREE ebook, *Escape & Evade*, at my website (AlexAnderNovelist.com).

Excerpt from *The Unsanctioned Patriot*

THE UNSANCTIONED PATRIOT

A PATRIOTIC ACTION THRILLER

ALEX ANDER

30 June—9:55 p.m. (local time)
Somewhere in the foothills
of the mountains in Nigeria

"Alpha's in position—over."

"Copy that, Alpha. Bravo, report."

"Bravo's in position—over."

"Copy that, Bravo. Charlie, what's your status?"

"Charlie is thirty seconds to ready—over."

Hidden high above the compound, Sergeant Aaron Hardy moved his legs and body as much as he could. He had been in the prone position for the last seventeen hours, and his muscles were cramping. In two days, he would celebrate his thirtieth birthday; however, at this moment, he felt twice that age.

Hardy had enlisted in the United States Marine Corps upon graduating from high school. He had spent the first four years of his career serving overseas, primarily in Iraq, before becoming a member of the Second Marine Special Operations Battalion, headquartered at Camp Lejeune, North Carolina. For the next five years, he had been involved in numerous direct-action, special reconnaissance, and counter-terrorism missions until he had been asked to command a team of his own and conduct top-secret missions all over the world.

Lately, Hardy had been considering a new line of work. During the last five years, his body had been under an extreme amount of stress, and he did not recover as quickly as he once did. He was still in great physical shape, but he knew if he maintained this breakneck speed, his body would fail much quicker. He still wanted to be part of Special Operations, just in a little less intense setting that did not require so much scouting. The countless hours spent waiting for the action were making him grow restless. And, in many ways, they took a greater toll on his body than did the gunfights. He wanted to see more action, and he wanted more control over the action. He wanted to take the fight to the enemy, not wait for the enemy to dictate the terms of engagement.

Hardy peered through his binoculars and scanned the area.

Milling around, two sentries guarded the main gate. Located in the center of the compound, the main building was dark and quiet. Fifty meters to the rear, two buildings—ten meters apart from each other—served as living quarters for the soldiers. Both structures were alive with activity. The men inside were raucous. Music blasted from one of the buildings.

80s punk rock, thought Hardy, lowering the binoculars to glimpse his watch. He raised the eyeglasses again, as his earpiece crackled.

     Excerpt from The Unsanctioned Patriot

"Overwatch, this is Charlie. We're in position awaiting your orders—over."

"Copy that." Hardy slowly swung the binoculars to the right. "All teams, standby."

Hardy checked his watch numerous times in the next few minutes. This was exactly what was making him grow restless—the waiting. His teams were in place, ready to carry out their tasks, but everything hinged on the target.

The voice of another team leader filled the airwaves. "Inbound vehicles eight hundred meters out and closing fast."

Finally. Through the field glasses, Hardy caught sight of the approaching headlights to his left. He watched two SUVs speed toward the compound and come to a stop outside the main gate. The guards opened the gate and waved them through.

Once the vehicles were at the main building, the second SUV's occupants jumped out and took defensive positions around the first SUV. Armed with AK-47 rifles, four men dressed in black suits, white shirts, and black ties stood guard. Their heads rotating left and right, they searched for security threats.

The driver and the front passenger of the first SUV, both similarly dressed and armed, hurried inside the main building. A few moments later, they emerged, stood on either side of the front door, and surveyed the landscape. The one to the left put his wrist to his mouth.

AK-47 in hand, a man got out of the left-rear door of the first SUV, hurried around the back bumper, and opened the right-rear passenger door.

Two feet swung around and landed on the ground. A second later, their owner—a Nigerian warlord—threw his upper body forward and rose to his feet. Nigerian oversaw the most powerful drug cartel in the country. He stood six-two and tipped the scales at more than three hundred pounds.

Hardy spun the wheel on the binoculars, zooming in on the man's face. He needed visual confirmation to proceed with the mission.

His back to Hardy, the man examined his surroundings. He buttoned his suit coat and took a few steps toward the main building before stopping.

"Come on," Hardy said under his breath. "Show me your face."

Continuing his journey, Nigerian turned his head.

Hardy's middle finger rotated the focus dial a hair, and his eyes narrowed. *Gotcha.* "All teams, this is Overwatch. We are a go. I repeat. All teams, we are a go on my command—over."

"Copy that," replied all three team leaders.

Hardy dropped his binoculars, wrapped his right hand around the stock of the M40A5 sniper rifle in front of him, and shouldered the weapon. He closed his left eye and acquired the two guards at the main gate through the rifle's scope. Swinging the rifle to the right, he placed

    Excerpt from The Unsanctioned Patriot

Nigerian in his crosshairs. When the man was two steps away from the front door of the building, Hardy had the two guards in the scope again. "Go, go, go!"

While the men from the SUVs fell to the ground, shot by his teammates, Hardy eased back his weapon's trigger. Two muffled 'pops' from his rifle later, the 7.62x51mm NATO bullets found their targets, and the sentries dropped.

"This is Alpha. All tangos are down. I repeat. All tangos are down—over."

Two massive explosions lit up the night sky, as the two structures to the rear of the main building blew apart. One huge fireball rose from the remains.

Hardy heard small arms fire before his earpiece came alive.

"This is Bravo. All tangos have been neutralized—over."

Hardy held his breath waiting for the next situation report.

Charlie Team had the most delicate part of the operation. Their orders were to secure Nigerian. They were to engage him only if he returned fire, and they were to shoot to incapacitate, not kill.

Balling his hand, Hardy called for a situation report. "Charlie, I need a sitrep—over." In his ear, he heard sporadic weapons' fire, team members shouting, scuffling. Moments later, the commotion stopped, and silence ensued.

"What's your sitrep, Charlie?" No response. "Bravo, advance on the main building. I repeat. Bravo—"

"Overwatch, this is Charlie."

Hardy squinted through the binoculars. "Bravo, stand down and await further orders. Go ahead, Charlie."

"Overwatch, we have your birthday present...all wrapped up and ready for delivery—over."

Hardy sighed. "Copy that. All teams rendezvous for evac." Hardy paused before letting a grin form on his face. "Good work, gentlemen. Let's go home."

Thirty minutes later, with his teams safely aboard two Bell UH-1Y Venom (Super Huey) helicopters, Hardy was the last man to board an aircraft and take his place among his men.

The choppers lifted off and banked left.

Feeling the tension drain from his shoulders, he hung his head and let out a slow, long breath. He had brought his people to the completion of another mission without any casualties. In twelve hours, everyone would be stateside enjoying some much needed rest and relaxation. He shut his eyes. *A good day.*

...

The Next Day...
1 July—8:46 P.M.
Washington, D.C.
Admiring the Federal Reserve Building on his left,

    Excerpt from The Unsanctioned Patriot

Aaron Hardy walked down Forty-First Street. It was good to be back on American soil, taking in the sights of Washington D.C. He was on his way to the restaurant to meet his entire team for drinks. In a few hours, Hardy would turn thirty, and his team was determined to celebrate this birthday milestone.

After the mission in Nigeria, everyone was excited to get out and blow off a little steam. The restaurant of choice was The Ole Town Tavern, a small and well-known establishment in the Downtown District of D.C. Its roots date back to the turn of the twentieth century. Arguably, the restaurant had the best shrimp on the East Coast.

Hardy tugged on the handle of a heavy glass door and stepped inside the eatery. The noise of a raucous crowd greeted him. He was immediately immersed in the atmosphere of patrons mixing food, alcohol, and sports. The place was packed with people cheering for their favorite team and downing a few too many beers. Hardy sidestepped servers and squeezed between tables, as he headed to the back of the building to a small room his team had reserved.

Hardy entered the room to an ovation of applause from his men. He saw several empty beer bottles on the table and snickered to himself. *I guess I'm late.*

He took off his jacket and draped the garment over an open chair. After listening to several good-natured comments about his age, and being told the next round of drinks was on him, he left to find the men's room.

Halfway down a narrow and dimly lit hallway, he stepped aside and nodded at two young women as they passed.

They gave him a flirtatious smile.

His cell phone rang, and he connected the call while watching the women.

They cranked their heads his way for another glance.

"Hello. This is Hardy. Hello?" The voice on the line was barely audible. "What? I can hardly—"

Something happened with the game on the television, and the people clapped and screamed.

After a quick look toward the noise, "Hold on a second," he found a nearby door at the back of the restaurant and slipped outside. As the door slowly shut behind him, he focused his attention on the call. "Okay, who's—"

The restaurant exploded, sending fragments of glass and brick flying through the air. The closing door slammed into his back. His head rocked backwards and bounced off the door before his body was thrown more than ten feet.

Landing near a metal dumpster, he rolled onto his side and saw flames shooting out of the tavern's upper windows. Heat from the fire singed the hairs on his arms while he crawled behind the dumpster. Lying on his back, the last thing he saw was the night sky and a full moon before a secondary explosion pushed the dumpster—and

Hardy—further away from the building.

9 798822 743453 1